W9-AXR-478

Veronica's First Year

by
Jean Sasso Rheingrover

Illustrations by
Kay Life

Albert Whitman & Company • Morton Grove, Illinois

In memory of Mom,
who listened with her heart;
in thanksgiving for my husband, Scott,
and our children, Daniel, Gregory, and Corey,
who bring love and joy to each day;
in celebration of Elizabeth,
who taught us all not to be afraid.   — J.S.R.

With warm thanks and gratitude to the family birthplace
at Providence Hospital, Holyoke, Massachusetts;
Debbie and her family; John and his family.   — K.G.L.

Design is by Lindaanne Donohoe.
The text typeface is Caxton.
The illustrations are rendered in watercolor.

Library of Congress Cataloging-in-Publication Data

Rheingrover, Jean Sasso.
Veronica's first year / written by Jean Sasso Rheingrover;
illustrated by Kay Life.
p.   cm.
Summary: Nine-year-old Nathan helps welcome his
baby sister, who has Down syndrome,
into the family and eagerly anticipates the day when
she will be able to ride his tricycle.
ISBN 0-8075-8474-6
[1. Down syndrome—Fiction. 2. Mentally handicapped—Fiction.
3. Brothers and sisters—Fiction. 4. Babies—Fiction.]
I. Life, Kay, ill. II. Title.
PZ7.R33785Ve   1996   95-52925
[E]—dc20   CIP
                                                  AC

Text copyright ©1996 by Regina M. Rheingrover.
Illustrations copyright ©1996 by Kay Life.
Published in 1996 by Albert Whitman & Company,
6340 Oakton Street, Morton Grove, Illinois 60053.
Published simultaneously in Canada by General Publishing, Limited, Toronto.
Printed in the United States of America.
10 9 8 7 6 5 4 3 2 1

Nathan waited a long time for Veronica to come. He watched Daddy paint her bedroom yellow like the buttercups that grew in the grass. He helped Mama hang up a mobile of zebras and panda bears above her crib. With his very own money, he bought her a red rubber bear that squeaked when you pressed its tummy.

Veronica was born at the end of the summer. She came when the last of the yellow jackets were stinging and the first of the crickets were singing. She came the week that the training wheels were taken off Nathan's bicycle and Nathan rode around the block by himself for the very first time.

Veronica arrived in the night, while Nathan slept. When he woke up, Mama and Daddy were gone and Grandma was sitting at the kitchen table. "Your mother has had the baby," Grandma whispered. "It's a little girl." There were tears on Grandma's face, and she pulled Nathan onto her lap and held him close.

Nathan wanted to see Veronica right away. Mama talked to him on the telephone. "Your little sister is a special baby," Mama said. "She may need extra help at the hospital. Daddy will bring you to see her as soon as he can."

Nathan wondered what made Veronica a special baby. He heard Daddy and Grandma talking about her. He heard the words *Down syndrome*. Nathan felt worried.

The next day after school, Daddy took Nathan to the hospital. It was wonderful to see Mama. She laughed when Nathan hugged her. She cried a little bit, too. Then she took his hand, and Mama and Daddy and Nathan went to the nursery to see Veronica.

Mama pointed to Veronica's bassinet, and Nathan stood up on his tiptoes to see her. Veronica was not crying like some of the babies. Her eyes were open, and as Nathan watched she wiggled inside her white cotton cocoon. A small fist poked into sight. Nathan waved to Veronica. "I think she sees me," he said, not taking his eyes from her tiny, silent face. Mama squeezed Nathan's hand. Daddy bent down and kissed his cheek.

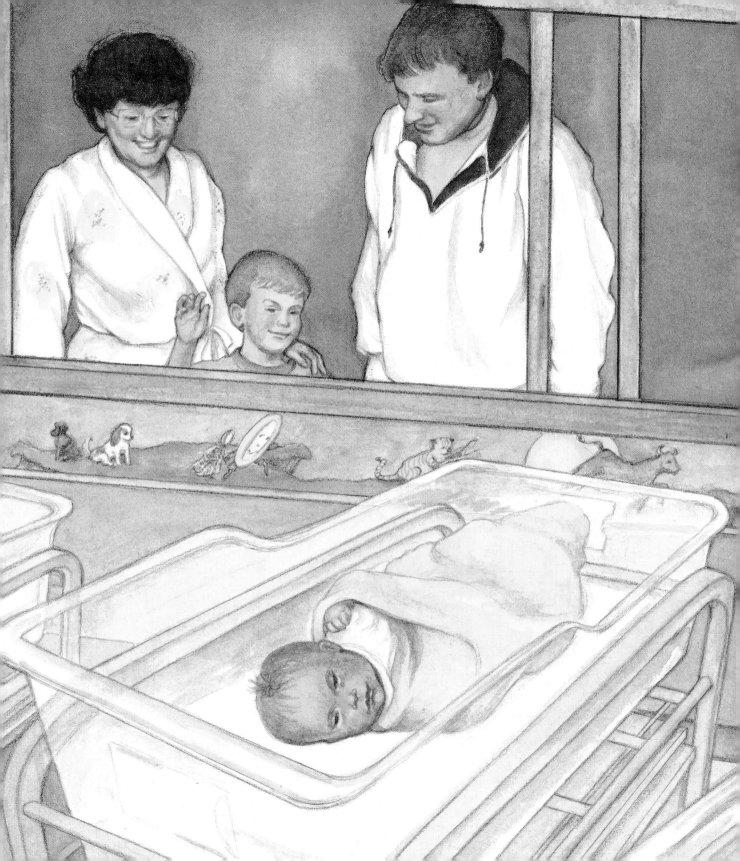

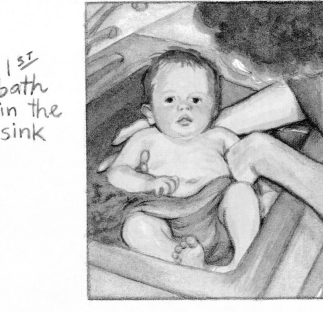

1ST bath in the sink

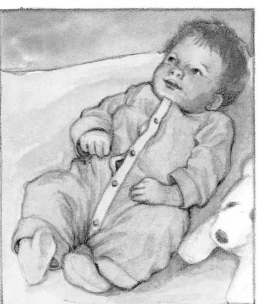

Look at me, I rolled over!

That night at bedtime, Daddy brought Nathan's baby album into his room. On the cover was one of Nathan's baby pictures and the words "Nathan's First Year." Together they looked at the pictures of Nathan when he was a baby. Daddy read the writing under the pictures.

Nathan always liked looking at his baby pictures. Tonight he especially liked the one of him taking a bath in the sink; it reminded him of Veronica.

6 months old

9 months old

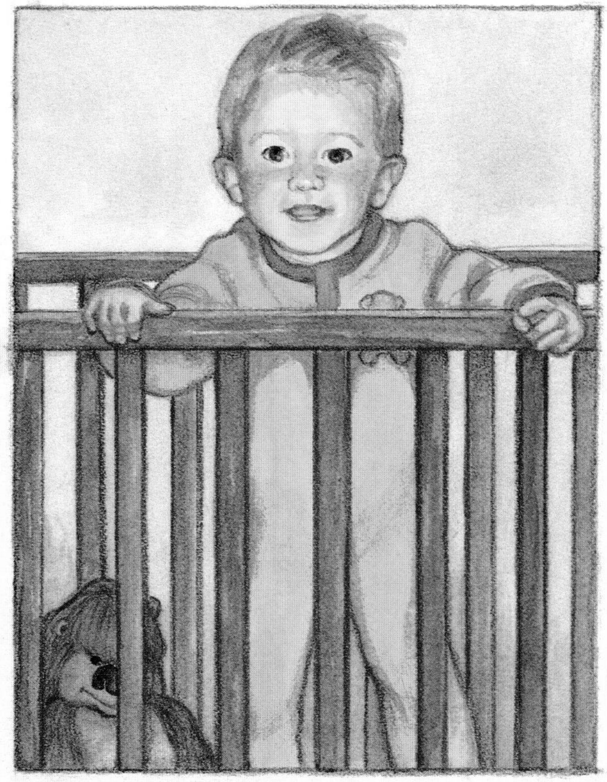

Sitting up
by myself

Standing in
the crib

12
months
old

I'm
walking!

Nathan woke up early the next morning. He found Daddy shaving in the bathroom.

"Is Veronica sick?" asked Nathan.

"No," answered Daddy. "Veronica is a baby with Down syndrome. That means that it will take her longer to learn how to do things. She will be older than you were when she learns how to sit up and stand in her crib and walk, but she will learn how to do all those things and many other things, too."

"I can help Veronica," said Nathan.

"Yes, you can," said Daddy. "We will all help her together. And that will start this morning, when you and I go to the hospital to bring Mama and Veronica home."

Later that day, Veronica and her family came home.

Daddy held the door for Mama and helped her up the steps.

Mama carried Veronica into her yellow room and gently laid her in her crib.

Reaching through the side of the crib, Nathan squeezed the red rubber bear. Veronica turned her head at the squeaking sound and kicked her legs.

"Look," said Nathan. "She wants to play." After a moment Nathan asked, "Will Veronica learn to ride bikes with me?"

"You know, Nathan," said Daddy, "I'm sure that she will."

One evening, Daddy brought home a new baby album. On the cover, he and Nathan pasted a picture of Nathan holding Veronica. With a pink marker they wrote the words "Veronica's First Year."

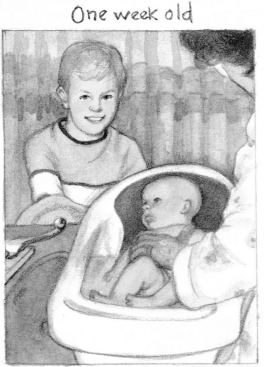

One week old

Three months old

I ˢᵗ Bath. Big brother is holding my towel.

What a happy face! Guess who I'm smiling at?

Every month new pictures were added to Veronica's baby album. Pictures of special times, like their vacation at the beach, and of everyday times, like walks in the neighborhood and visits to the park.

Soon the album was filled. Together, Mama and Nathan wrote under the pictures.

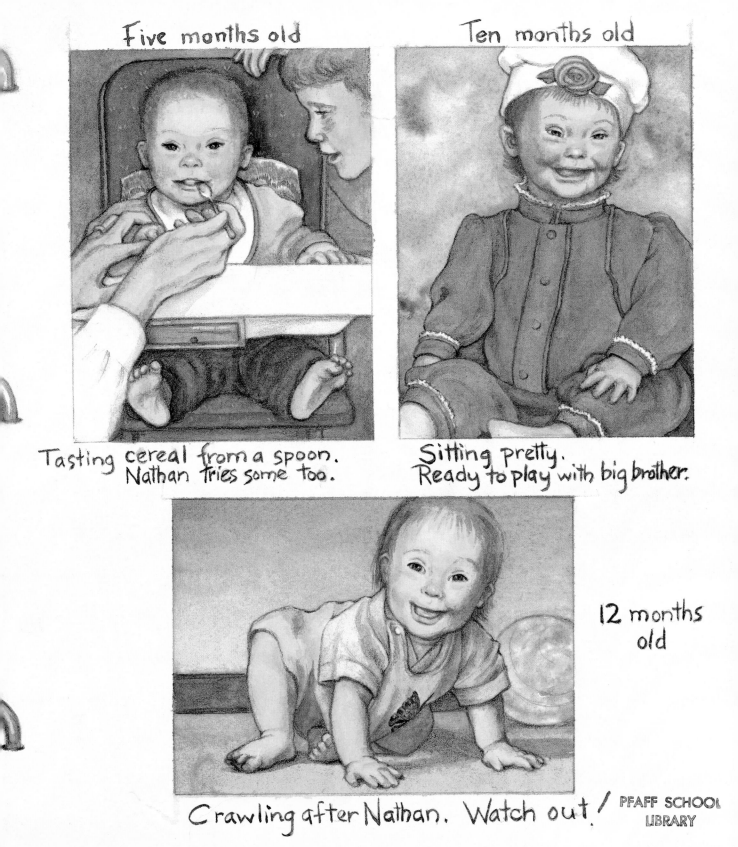

Five months old

Ten months old

Tasting cereal from a spoon.
Nathan tries some too.

Sitting pretty.
Ready to play with big brother.

12 months
old

Crawling after Nathan. Watch out!

Nathan liked all the pictures in Veronica's album. But one was his favorite. It showed Mama standing outside with Nathan and Veronica. Next to them was Nathan's tricycle, all shined up with a big bow on the handlebars. Underneath the picture was written:

"My first birthday. What a great present from a super big brother!"

Nathan always felt happy when he looked at that picture. He knew that someday Veronica really would ride his tricycle—and his bicycle, too.

Veronica's 1st Birthday

Down syndrome is a congenital syndrome, which means that it is present at birth. Individuals with Down syndrome have an extra chromosome. This results in a genetic imbalance which causes slower than average physical and mental development, though there is considerable variation from child to child.

Learning that their baby has Down syndrome can be very difficult for a family. Parents and grandparents are often sad and apprehensive. Other children in the family may wonder why people are distressed about an event that had been anticipated with joy.

It is helpful for parents to be open with their other children about the new baby, to listen to their concerns and questions, and to answer them honestly. It is important to remember that each baby with Down syndrome is a unique person, graced with his or her own personality, abilities, strengths and weaknesses, likes and dislikes.

As family and baby grow together, they will deepen in their understanding of themselves and each other. Each member of the family can come to know that being different is not something to be feared, but to be celebrated.

Help is available from doctors, therapists, teachers, and other parents of children with Down syndrome. Involvement in an early developmental intervention program will assist the baby with Down syndrome to develop to his or her fullest potential while providing necessary information and guidance to the family. Parent and sibling groups exist in most areas and can provide a supportive community.